PING-PING
THE PANDA

Jan Davis and Jon Resnick

TRUE-TO-LIFE BOOKS

Educating children about endangered species

Koala Books
www.koalabooks.com.au

Hi! My name is Ping-Ping and I am a giant panda. I live in the beautiful bamboo forests and rugged mountains of southwestern China.

Ping-Ping means 'peace' in Chinese. Pandas have long been a symbol of peace in China. Our cute, cuddly appearance has helped bring people together from around the world.

Do you think I look like a bear
or a raccoon? For over 100 years,
scientists weren't sure to which family
pandas belonged. New research shows
we are more closely related to bears.

Pandas would not survive without bamboo.
We spend up to 12 hours a day eating the stems
and leaves of different species. An adult will eat
around 12 kilograms of bamboo each day.

Can you see how I hold the bamboo when I eat? Pandas have a special thumb that lets us grasp things like a human hand. Our powerful jaws and sharp teeth also help us slice, crush and grind bamboo stems up to 40mm thick.

Pandas live alone in a home range of about four to six and a half square kilometres. We spend the day eating, grooming, scent marking and resting.

Like all bears, we love climbing trees.
It's fun, good exercise and helps us
escape from predators.

My distinctive black and white colouring
is world-famous. No other mammal
has the same markings as I do.
When I was born, I was completely white.
The black patches began to develop at
about ten days old.

Pandas make 11 different sounds.
Sometimes we cry like a baby; other times we bark
like a dog. Growls, honks, chirps and squeals are
just some of the other ways we communicate.

This is my cousin, Ring-Ring.
He is a red panda.

He lives in the same kind of habitat as I do.
He loves to eat bamboo too and spends a lot of
time in trees. Red pandas are also endangered.

Giant pandas are very rare.
Fewer than 1,000 of us survive in the wild.
Unfortunately, our future is uncertain.

Without immediate help, we will lose our
habitat and the bamboo we depend on.
Please show you care and bring
peace to the pandas.

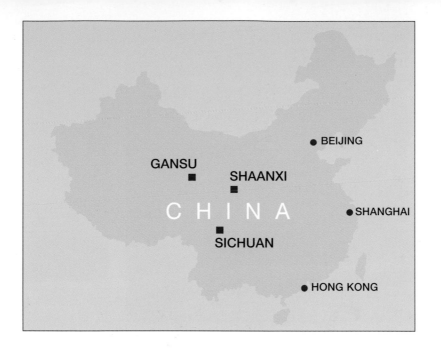

GIANT PANDA FACTS

SCIENTIFIC NAME
Ailuropoda melanoleuca (means black and white cat-footed).

HABITAT
Pandas are found only in southwestern China, in Sichuan, Gansu and Shaanxi provinces. They live at high altitudes (2,600 to 3,000 metres) in misty mountains with dense forests of conifer trees and bamboo.

WEIGHT
Up to 160 kilos (males are 10-20% heavier than females).

LENGTH
1.5 to 1.8 metres.

AT BIRTH
- Pandas weigh 90-130 grams at birth, about 900 times less than their mother.
- Cubs are born blind and can see after 6-8 weeks.
- They depend on mothers' milk.
- Cubs don't eat bamboo until they are 13-14 months old.

DIET
Pandas rely on up to 25 species of bamboo for 99% of their diet. Also known to eat other plants, flowers, mushrooms, fish and rodents. Usually drink water once a day.

PREDATORS
Only humans. They destroy the pandas' habitat and kill individuals to sell their valuable skin.

LIFE SPAN
Up to 20 years in the wild and 30 years in captivity.

NUMBERS REMAINING (estimate)
GIANT PANDA. Fewer than 1,000 (last survey was 1988)
RED PANDA. Uncertain, one estimate is fewer than 25 in the wild, 336 in captivity.

DID YOU KNOW?
- Pandas have been on Earth for over 3 million years.
- Once the pandas' range extended into Myanmar and Vietnam.
- Westerners first discovered pandas in 1869.
- From time to time, large areas of bamboo will flower and then die off.
- Pandas have poor eyesight but a good sense of smell.
- The red panda is about the size of a house cat, but is more closely related to a raccoon.

SUGGESTED READING

GIANT PANDA (Animals in Danger)
Rod Theodorou, 2000

LITTLE PANDA: THE WORLD WELCOMES
HUA MEI AT THE SAN DIEGO ZOO
Joanne Ryder, 2001

PANDAS (World Life Library)
Heather Angel, 1998

PANDAS FOR KIDS (Wildlife for Kids Series)
Kathy Feeney, 1997

SAVING THE GIANT PANDA
Terry L. Maple, 2000

SMITHSONIAN BOOK OF GIANT PANDAS
Susan Lumpkin, John Seider, John
Seidensticker, 2002

THE GIANT PANDA
(Endangered Animals & Habitats)
Judith Janda Presnall, 1998

THE LAST PANDA
George Schaller, 1993

THE LEGEND OF THE PANDA
Linda Granfield, 1998

THE PANDA: WILD ABOUT BAMBOO
(Animal Close-ups)
Valerie Tracqui, 1999

INTERESTING WEBSITES

ABSOLUTE PANDAS
www.everwonder.com/david/panda

ANIMAL PLANET
http://animal.discovery.com

CARE2
http://panda.care2.com

ENCHANTED LEARNING
www.zoomschool.com/subjects/mammals/panda

KIDS' PLANET
www.kidsplanet.org

NATIONAL GEOGRAPHIC
www.nationalgeographic.com/kids

SAN DIEGO ZOO
www.sandiegozoo.org/special/pandas/index.html

THE SMITHSONIAN NATIONAL ZOO
http://pandas.si.edu

WORLD WILDLIFE FUND
www.worldwildlife.org/pandas

WORLD WIDE FUND FOR NATURE
www.panda.org/resources/publications/species/pandas